Ann Tompert

Nothing Sticks Like a Shadow

Illustrated by Lynn Munsinger

Houghton Mifflin Company Boston 1984

Library of Congress Cataloging in Publication Data

Tompert, Ann.
    Nothing sticks like a shadow.

    Summary: To win a bet, Rabbit tries to get rid of his shadow,
with the aid of many animal friends.
    [1. Shadows — Fiction. 2. Animals — Fiction]
I. Munsinger, Lynn, ill. II. Title.
PZ7.T598No   1984   [E]   83-18554
ISBN 0-395-35391-2

P 10 9 8 7 6 5 4 3 2 1

Nothing Sticks
Like a Shadow

One day Rabbit was dancing a wild fandango in a field filled with clover. Woodchuck was watching him from the doorway of his burrow.

"Isn't it lonely, playing by yourself?" Woodchuck asked.

"I'm not alone," said Rabbit, pointing. "See my shadow? It goes where I go and does what I do."

"I know what you mean," said Woodchuck.
"I can't escape my shadow either, no matter how hard I try."

"I can if I want to," said Rabbit.

"Oh, no, you can't," said Woodchuck. "No one can."

"I can too," said Rabbit.

"Can't," said Woodchuck.

And they pitched "cans" and "can'ts" at each other until Woodchuck said, "I'll bet you my hat you can't."

"Looks as if I'm going to have a new hat," said Rabbit. He ran and hid behind the trunk of a huge tree.

When he looked around, however, he found his shadow
standing beside him.

Woodchuck laughed. "You'll have to do better than that,"
he said.

Rabbit hurried over to a bunch of bushes and hid behind them. He looked around. No shadow did he see. "I've lost it!" he cried, peeking from behind the bushes at Woodchuck. "Give me your hat."

"Oh, no, you haven't," said Woodchuck, pointing.

Rabbit looked to where Woodchuck was pointing and saw his shadow's head peeking from behind the bushes, too.

"Take my advice," said Woodchuck. "Give it up. Stop wasting time. Nothing sticks like a shadow."

With this, he went into his burrow.

"Woodchuck thinks he knows everything," Rabbit said to his shadow. "But I'll show him. I'll run away from you."

And with a great leap, he set out across the field of clover.

Rabbit took longer and longer leaps. His shadow took longer and longer leaps as it followed right behind him.

Soon Rabbit came to a path beside a river. There he met Beaver carrying a broom over his shoulder.

"Why are you running?" asked Beaver.

"I'm trying to get away from my shadow," said Rabbit. "Woodchuck bet me his hat that I couldn't."

"Well," said Beaver, "it's easy to see you can't run away from it. See if you can sweep it away. Nothing sweeps better than a new broom, you know, and I just bought this one at the market."

"Thank you," said Rabbit.

And he began to sweep the path where his shadow lay.

Back and forth, back and forth, Rabbit swished the broom. Great whirlwinds of dust filled the air. Soon Rabbit was coated with dust. Dust got into his eyes, making them itch. Dust got into his nose. He sneezed, and then he sneezed again. But he didn't stop sweeping until he could see his shadow no longer.

"I've lost it!" he cried. "I've lost it!"

Dropping his broom, Rabbit danced a little jig. As he danced, the dust settled to the ground. And there was his shadow dancing beside him.

"I guess shadows can't be swept away," said Beaver. "I'm sorry I couldn't help you." He picked up his broom and went on his way.

No sooner had Beaver left than Skunk came along.

"Goodness!" he exclaimed. "What happened? I've never seen anyone so dirty."

"I was trying to sweep my shadow away," said Rabbit.

"Everyone knows you can't sweep away shadows," said Skunk.

"You can't hide from them or run away from them either," said Rabbit.

"Right," said Skunk. "When two things are stuck together, you must pull them apart."

He leaned over, grabbed Rabbit and pulled.

Nothing happened. He grabbed Rabbit again and jerked
so hard that he tumbled over backward.

Skunk was ready to try a third time when along came Fox on her way to a meeting of her Sewing Circle. "What in the world is going on?" she asked.

"I'm trying to pull Rabbit away from his shadow," said Skunk.

"Woodchuck bet me his hat that I can't get away from it," said Rabbit.

Fox looked at the shadow carefully. Then she took her scissors from her sewing basket. "Some things are too hard to tear apart," she said. "Let me see if I can cut Rabbit's shadow loose."

Clip, clip, clip, Fox went with her scissors. *Clip, clip, clip*.
Nothing happened.

Fox was still clipping when Raccoon came along.

"Well, well," Raccoon said. "What do we have here?"

"I'm trying to get rid of my shadow," Rabbit said.

"Why?" asked Raccoon. "Shadows are handy things to have. Sometimes they show you where you are going, and sometimes they show you where you've been."

"I know," said Rabbit. "But Woodchuck bet me his hat that I can't get rid of mine even if I want to."

"Did you try hiding from it?" asked Raccoon.

"Yes," said Rabbit. "But it didn't work. And I couldn't run away from it or sweep it away."

"I couldn't cut it off," said Fox.

"Let's try soaking it off," said Raccoon. And he ushered Rabbit to the river's edge.

Rabbit put one foot into the water, then jerked it out.

"It's cold!" he wailed.

"Go on," urged Raccoon.

Rabbit took a step.

"Keep going," said Raccoon.

Rabbit shivered. "It's too cold!" he cried.

He swung around to leave the river, bumped into Raccoon, and fell into the water with a great splash. The river swirled around him. He tossed and rolled, trying to get back to his feet.

Raccoon grabbed him and dragged him to shore. Rabbit was wet to the skin. Water dripped from his ears. His clothes hung on him like wet rags. Never had he felt so miserable. But the water had not washed away his shadow. There it was beside him.

"Looks as if you're stuck with your shadow," said Raccoon.

"Why don't you give up?" asked Fox.
"Tell Woodchuck he's right," said Skunk.
"I don't want to," said Rabbit. "But I guess I'll have to."
Rabbit walked slowly across the fields.

When he reached Woodchuck's burrow, Woodchuck was not at home. Rabbit stretched out on a flat sunny rock to wait for him. His shadow stretched out beside him. He was tired. The hot sun felt good. Soon steam rose from his drying clothes. He thought about moving to a shady spot, but he was too sleepy to do so.

"Anyway," he said with a yawn, "if I stay here, maybe the sun will melt my shadow away."

Rabbit tried hard to keep his eyes open to watch the sun melt his shadow. But his eyelids grew heavier and heavier until he fell asleep.

It was dark when Woodchuck shook Rabbit awake. "You win," said Woodchuck.

Rabbit yawned and stretched and rubbed the sleep from his eyes.

Woodchuck put his hat on Rabbit's head. "Congratulations," he said. "Your shadow is gone."

Rabbit turned round and round. "Oh, dear," he wailed. "The sun *did* melt my shadow."

"That's what you wanted, isn't it?" asked Woodchuck.

"No," wailed Rabbit. "I was only trying to show you that I could get rid of it if I wanted to. And now it's gone! What am I going to do without it?"

At that moment, the clouds parted. A full moon shone. And there was Rabbit's shadow.

"Look!" cried Rabbit. "It's back! You were right after all."

And he and his shadow whirled and twirled in a wild fandango.

"Of course I'm right," crowed Woodchuck, snatching his hat from Rabbit's head. "I told you that nothing sticks like a shadow."